YOU ARE ABOUT TO SET OFF ON AN ADVENTURE WITH

INDIANA JONES™

—A JOURNEY TO THE SNOWY PEAKS OF THE HIMALAYA MOUNTAINS.

Will you and Indy really find the legendary Silver Tower that is hidden in these mountains? What strange and terrifying creatures will attempt to block your path? Can you survive your visit to the Village of Giants?

On your journey with Indy you will choose your own actions and decide your own fate by following the directions at the bottom of each page.

If you make the right choices, your many adventures in this book will be exciting—and successful.

If you make the wrong choices, you and Indy may be trapped in those frozen mountains forever!

Be careful...and good luck!

INDIANA JONES
JONES ™
and the
GIANTS OF THE SILVER TOWER

by R.L. Stine

Illustrated by DAVID B. MATTINGLY

SPHERE BOOKS LIMITED
London and Sydney

First published in Great Britain by
Sphere Books Ltd 1984
30–32 Gray's Inn Road, London WC1X 8JL
Copyright © 1984 Lucasfilm Ltd. (LFL)
TM: 'Find Your Fate' is a Trademark of Random House,
Inc.
'Indiana Jones' is a Trademark of Lucasfilm Ltd.
Used under authorisation.
This edition published by arrangement with Ballantine Books,
A Division of Random House, Inc.

Designed by Gene Siegel

Cover and interior art by David B. Mattingly

Printed and bound in Great Britain by
Cox & Wyman Ltd, Reading

INDIANA JONES™
and the
GIANTS OF THE SILVER TOWER

Find Your Fate™ Adventure #3

Nepal, 1933

"Watch out, kid!" Indiana Jones yells. But his warning comes too late.

You bump right into the lead porter. He cries out in surprise and drops the large wooden crate he is carrying. The other porters laugh as you try to apologize.

"I was looking at the mountains. I didn't watch where I was going," you say.

"He can't understand you, kid," Indy says. "You're pretty far from home, you know. Most people in the foothills of the Himalayas don't speak English."

The Himalayas! The tallest mountains in the world!

When your parents sent you to stay with your cousin Indiana Jones for the summer, they had little idea that you and Indy would soon be heading toward Nepal—and the Himalaya Mountains!

Now you and Indy stand in the small camp on a high grassy plain, waiting for the porters and Sherpas to ready your supplies. You look out over a wide forest of tall trees, and then beyond, to where all vegetation stops and the incredible mountains climb white and frozen into the clouds.

The wind picks up, still wet from the monsoon that has just passed. You tighten the sheepskin hood around your head.

"Oh, I don't believe it!" a voice cries.

It is a woman's voice. What is the problem?

....

Quick—go on to page 2.

1

"I just don't believe we'll *ever* find my father up there in those mountains!" Lilah Rogers cries. "I never should have dragged you up here, Indy."

Indy looks uncomfortable. You realize he isn't too good at reassuring people. "It's worth a try, Lilah," he says quietly, his eyes on the mountains.

"We are ready now, sahib," says Mohaji, the short, dark leader of the Sherpas. He smiles at you. "The young one is brave to make such a journey."

"With you leading us, Mohaji, the journey will be an easy one," Indy says. Mohaji smiles again, enjoying the flattery. "We're on our way, kid," Indy says, turning to you.

"On our way?" you repeat, your voice shaking just a bit.

"On our way to the Roof of the World!" Indy says.

What is Lilah's father doing up in those mountains? And why are the three of you heading up after him?

Turn to page 21 to find out.

The four of you wander out into the frozen night. A full moon lights the sky and casts a soft glow on the snow before you. It crunches beneath your boots as you walk quickly, trying to stay up with Indy, Lilah, and her father.

"The blizzard was absolutely blinding," George tells Indy. "But I've always had an excellent sense of direction. I've dreamed the way back to that tower every night. I know I can find it."

You wander all night, sometimes following a trail left by merchants' caravans, sometimes making your own trail. Always climbing, climbing, climbing up to the top of the world.

And then, when you think you cannot take another step, when you feel frozen to the bone, too weary to move—

—THERE IT IS!

The Silver Tower of the Giants is real! And you are standing in front of it!

But you have no time to enjoy the sight. A dozen giants, the biggest people you have ever seen, climb out from behind the tall pine trees. They are dressed in silver furs that shine under the sun. Their angry voices echo loudly off the mountains. They pick up the four of you, nearly crushing you in their powerful arms. And they drag you off roughly to their village.

....
Turn to page 19.

You open your eyes. You try to focus.

It's Indy. He's leaning over you. "I knew you'd come around!" he says happily. You see Lilah standing behind Indy with a big smile on her face.

"Are we in heaven?" you ask groggily.

"Not unless heaven is a jungle," Indy says, his smile fading. "We've landed in the Nepalese jungle, kid. We didn't even make it to the mountains. The trees and soft ground of the jungle are the only reason we're alive. Sorry to say, the pilot didn't survive the fall."

You try to sit up, but you're still too dizzy.

"We have a choice to make now," Indy says.

"I choose to be anywhere but here," Lilah says.

"That's not one of the choices," Indy says. "Do we stay in this wrecked plane? Maybe someone saw us and will come rescue us. Or do we try our luck in this jungle? There's a chance we can find our way toward the mountains, where the Sherpas and porters will be waiting for us."

"We can't survive in this jungle," Lilah says. "I vote for staying here."

"Whaddaya say, kid?" Indy asks, turning to you.

....
Stay in the safety of the plane? Turn to page 22.

Take your chances in the jungle? Turn to page 15.

4

A few moments later you are standing before this astounding structure. "It's made of pure silver!" you say excitedly.

You have been discovered. A group of giants comes running out to greet you. They are at least eight feet tall and wear their hair in long black braids. Indy begins to say something to them, but the giants ignore him. They pick you up on their shoulders and carry you to the center of their village.

They put a crown on your head.

Then these giant men and women bow down to you. You are their king!

Turn to page 30.

The climb up the mountain to the Silver Tower is steep and difficult, but it goes very quickly. As you stand before the glowing silver structure, you are all too excited and too filled with awe to speak. The tower rises like a skyscraper, its top disappearing into the clouds.

The silence is broken by a greeting party of giants.

"They really are giants!" you yell, staring at these men who approach, men eight feet tall, wearing big, silver fur parkas, moving toward you with long strides.

"We've found the tower," Indy says, staring into the angry faces of the powerful men who approach. "But we may live to regret our discovery here!"

Turn to page 28.

"The snow is falling! Catch it! Catch it!" the man screams, and falls at Lilah's feet.

"Dad! It's you!" Lilah cries.

But George Rogers has collapsed in the snow. You and Indy quickly put up a tent and start a fire. You get Lilah's father warmed up and force some hot soup down his throat.

"The silver! It's falling from the sky!" he cries when he revives.

"He's half-starved and half out of his mind," Indy says softly, pouring a cup of steaming coffee. "I'm happy we found your father for you, Lilah. But he's in no shape to lead us to the Silver Tower." Indy sips the coffee slowly, his eyes unable to hide his disappointment.

"Yes, I can," George says.

You all turn to stare at Lilah's dad.

"It isn't far from here, actually," he says, and then drifts into a deep sleep.

Has George lost his mind in the snow? Or will he really be able to lead you to the Silver Tower? That's what all three of you wonder—as you look up and see an army of men heading straight for you!

Turn to page 36.

7

"Have you decided how you will travel, sa-hib?" Mohaji, the leader of the Sherpas, asks Indy.

"We must decide now," Indy says.

Behind you the porters are chanting a hymn for good luck as they wait to begin the journey. The music is strange, eerie. It reminds you that you are a long way from home.

"We have to cross the mountains," Indy says, "to get to the Tibetan side. That's where Lilah and George Rogers began their trip."

"Are we going to take that little plane?" you ask, pointing to the tiny, twin-engined prop plane at the edge of the grass.

8

"I do not recommend it, sahib," says Mohaji, his dark eyes staring intensely into Indy's. "The monsoon has passed us down here. But there still are storms up in the mountains. Better to allow me to lead you on foot."

"But we've *got* to take the plane! It's so much faster!" Lilah cries. "Dad has been up there for weeks already!"

This is your first big decision. Should you try to fly to the Tibetan side of the mountains—or follow Mohaji and his men on foot?

If you choose the plane, turn to page 26.
If you choose to go on foot, turn to page 50.

"How do you expect me to walk with all this stuff on my back?" Lilah asks.

"You don't have to walk. You can crawl, if you prefer," Indy says, tightening the giant pack on her back. "This'll help keep you warm." He loops a rope around his waist and hands it to you. "Loop it around you once, kid, then hand it to Lilah."

You do as he says. "Look—it stopped snowing!" you cry, looking out the small window.

"Things are looking brighter every minute," Indy says. "Maybe we'll find a hot dog stand on the corner."

"Okay. I'm ready," Lilah says, struggling to stand up under the weight of her supply pack. "Let's get going."

"Follow me," Indy says.

You step out of the broken plane into the blinding white of the Himalayan snows.

Turn to page 25.

You take turns keeping the fire going all night. Even with the blazing fire, the cave grows cold by morning. You wake up stiff and sore, eager to move on.

Lilah and her father have been awake for a while. They are standing on the other side of the fire, talking in loud whispers. They both seem to be upset. "I can't do it. I just can't do it!" you hear George say.

"Do what?" Indy asks impatiently.

George and Lilah walk slowly over to Indy. "I'm afraid we have a confession to make," Lilah says reluctantly. "I know you're going to hate me for this—but there *is* no Silver Tower or Village of Giants!"

Turn to page 23.

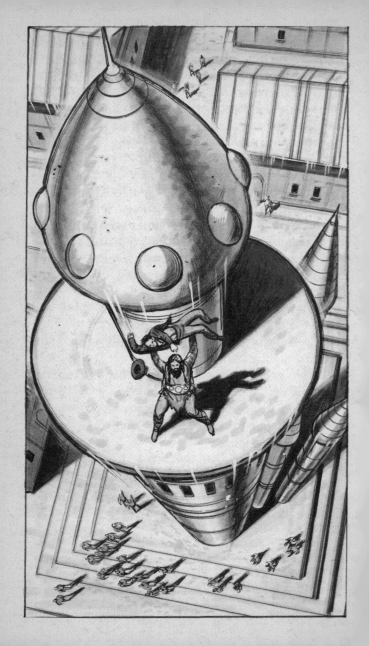

The giant warrior holds Indy high above his head. The giants cheer in anticipation of victory.

Indy's whip falls off his shoulder as the giant spins him around. You watch as the whip drops to the ground.

Will Indy drop right after it?

You feel sick at the thought.

Lilah and her father stand silently beside you, staring up to the top of the tower, hoping for a miracle.

Indy is reaching down now, trying to grab the giant's face but grabbing at nothing but air. Still holding Indy above his head, the giant backs up, first one step, then another, until both giant and his captive are out of view.

Everyone watches in silence now. Has the giant backed up to get a running start before tossing Indy off the tower? Has Indy forced the giant to back up?

No one can see what is happening up there.

Suddenly the silence is broken by a scream.

Everyone on the ground stares up at the tower, waiting for someone to step forward as the victor.

Has the giant thrown Indy to his death from the top of the glowing Silver Tower?

Turn to page 94.

13

"What is the problem?" Indy asks angrily. "I have paid you well."

"There is no payment high enough to make a Sherpa face what awaits this expedition," Mahaji says solemnly, staring into Indy's eyes.

"Answer my question," Indy persists. "What is the problem?"

"There is word, sahib, that a yeti awaits along the trail you have chosen to take. The men do not wish to take this trail. They do not wish to encounter the yeti in this lifetime."

"A yeti?" you ask. "Does he mean an Abominable Snowman?" You feel a thrill of fear. According to legend, yetis are half-human, half-apelike creatures twice the size of normal humans.

"This isn't good news, kid," Indy says, gesturing for you to keep quiet. "Listen, Mohaji, I picked the shortest route through these mountains."

"According to the men, the longer route is the one we must take, sahib," Mohaji says. "It is a more treacherous road, but it does not lead to the yeti."

You must decide what to do now.

....

Do you force the Sherpas and porters to take the shorter, safer route despite their fears? If so, turn to page 27.

Or do you agree to take the longer route? If so, turn to page 59.

14

"There may not be anyone in this jungle for a hundred miles," Indy says. "Pack up. We'll take as many supplies as we can. And let's get out of here!"

A few minutes later you are making your way through the vines and tall trees of the Nepalese jungle. Large, brightly colored birds caw overhead, and animals call and roar in the distance.

"It's just like a jungle in the movies," you say, trying to sound cheerful.

"It's real enough," Indy mutters.

Suddenly it becomes *too* real—as an immense roaring tiger leaps into your path!

Turn to page 72.

Blaaam!

Indy fires the pistol once. Twice.

The roar of the hoofbeats in deafening now. You can't decide whether to cover your ears— or your eyes!

Blaaam!

You close your eyes.

Blaaam! Blaaam!

You can't hear anything now . The roar of the stampeding yaks even drowns out the sound of Indy's pistol shots. You close your eyes tighter. Maybe, you think, when you open them, you will be back home, safe in bed, and it will have all turned out to be a noisy, bad dream.

Suddenly you realize that the roar of hoofbeats is getting softer. You open your eyes.

"It worked!" Indy cries, relief brightening his face. "They turned to the right!"

You don't have long to celebrate.

Now there is a roar coming from another direction—above you! You look up to the high peaks above the plateau. All three of you scream as you see the snow cascading down the peaks.

AVALANCHE!

Turn to page 37.

16

You open your eyes. You try to focus.

"It's cold," you say.

"Yeah, it's cold." You hear Indy's voice. "The front of the plane broke off. That accounts for the draft in here, kid."

You struggle to sit up. Lilah pulls herself up beside you. "We're okay!" she says, her voice soft with surprise.

"We're okay. The pilot isn't," Indy says, rubbing his arm through his sheepskin coat. "Afraid he didn't make it. It's just the three of us."

"Where are we?" you ask. You realize immediately that it's a dumb question, but you're still feeling a little dazed.

"We're either on some snow-covered peak on the Tibetan side of the Himalayas—or we're in heaven," Indy says, still rubbing his sore arm. "Oww. I really prefer softer landings."

"We're going to die here. I know it," Lilah says.

....
Go on to page 18.

17

"Try not to be so optimistic," Indy says. "*Someone* must be looking out for us; the plane crashed into snow, not into solid rock."

"Shall we go out and explore?" you ask.

"It's a lot colder out there than it is in here, kid," Indy says.

"Are you suggesting that we just wait inside this beat-up tin can till someone finds us?" Lilah asks.

"Well...we have a decision to make," Indy says, peering out at the snow. "It's warmer and safer inside what's left of this plane. If someone saw us go down, they'll come for us. On the other hand...if no one saw us, we'd be smarter to get out, take as many supplies as we can, and try to find a village or a monastery or something."

You must decide: stay in the plane? Or take your chances in the snow?

....
If you want to stay, turn to page 34.
If you want to go out, turn to page 10.

They carry you past their stone huts to the center of their village. Then they toss you to the ground.

"George, I don't think they're too glad to see us!" Indy says, groaning in pain.

"We never should've come back here," Lilah cries.

"But look at this amazing village!" says Indy. "What a discovery!"

"Quiet, everyone. I can communicate with them," George says. He sits up and calls out a few words in their language.

The giants' leader steps forward. He is at least eight feet tall, and the high fur hat he wears on his head makes him seem even taller. He has a long black braid that hangs behind him down to his waist. You can tell he is muscular and strong even through the heavy furs he wears as protection against the cold.

The giant's voice comes from deep within him as he speaks to George. His words seem to echo before they leave his mouth. George doesn't say a word. As he listens to the giant his face grows pale and frightened.

"I have some bad news," George says finally. "He wants to kill us all."

....

Turn to page 51.

It all started on the day of your arrival at Marshall College, where Indiana Jones is a professor of archeology. You were unpacking your small suitcase in Indy's rooming house when there was a knock on the door.

It was Lilah Rogers.

"Lilah! You look terrible!" was Indy's friendly greeting.

She ignored it. She had no time for greetings. She needed Indy's help.

"My father, Indy—he..."

Indy tossed some books off a wooden chair and motioned for Lilah to sit down. She slumped into the chair, then leaned forward nervously as she started her story again.

"My father and I were in the Himalayas in Tibet," she said. "He had a writing assignment from *Travel* magazine. It paid well enough for me to come along as his assistant.

"Dad and I followed a caravan trail for a while. But then we got lost. We wandered for days. We were so foolish to go on our own. It was snowing so hard, we couldn't see. I didn't think we'd make it."

"But you made it," Indy said impatiently.

"I made it. I don't know about Dad," Lilah said.

The rest of her story was astounding—even to Indiana Jones!

To hear more, turn to page 39.

21

"We have enough supplies in the plane to last us for—" Indy starts to say. But then he stops. "Hey—did you feel that?"

"Yeah," you say. "I thought maybe it was just me. I'm still feeling a little wobbly."

"I felt it too," Lilah says, fear creeping into her voice. "The plane moved."

The plane moves again as she says the words.

"It—it's sinking!" you cry. "The soft ground can't hold it!"

The plane lurches forward, its nose buried in muck now. "Grab whatever supplies you can," Indy says, making sure his bullwhip is around his shoulder. "And let's clear out of here!"

A few moments later the three of you, with supplies strapped to your backs, step out of the plane. You take a few steps—

—and sink to your waists in the marshy, soft jungle sand!

....
Turn to page 64.

"Please don't hate me, Indy," Lilah says, "but Dad and I didn't really find the Silver Tower or any village of giants. I told you we had found the tower to get you to help rescue Dad. I didn't trust anyone else to do it. And I knew you'd never come unless there was some kind of exciting project for you here."

"That's true," Indy says grimly. He is so disappointed he can barely talk. "And the coin? What about the silver coin?"

"It's a worthless fake. That's why I only let you look at it for a few seconds," Lilah says, unable to look Indy in the eye. "I'm sorry, Indy. Really I am." She puts a hand on Indy's shoulder.

Suddenly Indy's frowning face begins to brighten. "Don't be sorry," he says cheerfully.

"You're not angry? Why?" Lilah asks, completely surprised.

Indy's attention has turned away from her. "The cavemen!" he exclaims. "Just look at them! These prehistoric types are a better discovery than any tower! What a fabulous find! Now we've just gotta figure out how to sneak a couple of them onto the boat back home!"

You all have a good laugh, for now you know that this story has come to a happy

END.

The shovels from outside keep scraping away, tunneling through the thick snow.

"We're in here! We're in here!" you cry happily.

But your happiness turns to horror when you see your rescuers. The man with the red moustache is the first to break through the snow into the cave!

The bandit leader screams in triumph, his eyes wild in victory. Indy leaps at him, but the bandit dodges out of the way. He lifts his shovel.

"Look out, Indy!" you call.

But your warning is too late. The bandit brings the shovel down on Indy's head. Indy hits the ground and doesn't move.

You make a move toward Indy's bullwhip. But you realize you are now surrounded by bandits—bandits carrying rifles. The bandit leader throws back his head and laughs.

You had best close the book while he is still laughing. You really don't want to know the gruesome details of what happens when his laughter ends!

THE END

"Give your eyes a moment to adjust," Indy says, shielding his eyes with his arm.

"This is incredible!" Lilah says behind you.

"Hey—are you sure we're in the mountains?" you ask. "Look how flat it is!"

"We're on some sort of plateau," Indy says. "Well, that'll make it easier for a while. But we've got to start going down eventually—"

He stops and listens. A rumble in the distance.

"Is that thunder?" you ask.

"No. Not at this altitude," he says. "And not with clear, blue skies. Shhh. It's getting louder."

"It's an earthquake!" Lilah cries. "The whole mountain is shaking! I can feel it."

The ground does seem to be shaking. Indy stares straight ahead toward the direction of the strange rumbling.

"Hoofbeats!" you cry.

And you are right.

"Yaks!" Indy cries. "It's a stampede!"

The giant beasts are running at top speed across the snowy plateau, steam pouring from their nostrils, hoofbeats pounding against the snow—and they are heading right at you!

Turn to page 82.

The porters load as much of the supplies as they can onto the small plane. Indy pays their leader and turns toward the plane.

"I warn you. Don't go in that airplane, sahib," Mohaji calls to him. "Last night in my dream a bird fell from the sky. It is a warning, I fear."

"You'll have better dreams tonight," Indy tells him. "Come on, kid, Lilah. We've got mountains to cross."

The three of you climb into the tiny cabin. It is so cramped, you can't move without bumping into something or someone. Indy gives a signal to the pilot. The engine sputters and stalls. A pause. Then it sputters again and starts to roar. Outside the little window you can see the propellers begin to spin.

"This is going to be exciting," you say.

But you don't realize just *how* exciting!

Turn to page 32.

"I am very sorry, Mohaji," Indy tells the Sherpa, "but we must stick to our route. If we take the longer route, we run the risk of getting into heavy snowstorms. I want this trip to be as short as possible."

"We must find my dad quickly!" adds Lilah. "We can't take a longer route because of some silly superstition!"

"Superstition?" says Mohaji, his face growing even more somber. "The yeti is no superstition, miss."

"We can't discuss it any longer," Indy tells Mohaji. "Tell your men that we will keep to our original plans."

"Okay, sahib," Mohaji says quietly. "But I cannot guarantee that my men will stay with you for the entire journey."

"I'm willing to take that risk," Indy says defiantly. "Now, let's get this show on the road!"

A few moments later you, Indy, Lilah, and the Sherpas set off into the mountains. Have you made the right choice? Will you encounter the legendary yeti? And if so, will you survive the encounter?

Turn to page 62.

27

The leader of the giants steps forward, covered in silver furs that stretch down to the ground and trail behind him as he walks. He is a red-faced man with black eyes that seem to pierce right through you as he looks down at you. Angrily, he yells something at you in a strange language.

To your surprise, Indy replies in the same language.

The giants are as surprised as you that Indy can speak their language. "Don't look so shocked, kid," Indy mutters to you. "I *had* to pick up a *few* useful things in all my travels."

"But what did he say?" you ask eagerly.

"He said that his people do not like intruders," Indy says grimly.

The giant leader utters something else to Indy, his voice full of menace. Then he turns to discuss your fate with his comrades.

The four of you wait in silence. It seems like hours, and then finally the leader turns back to you. With a flat expression on his face that reveals nothing, he talks to Indy.

"Well?" Lilah asks, pulling at Indy's sleeve.

"He's going to allow us into his village," says Indy, his serious face slowly brightening. "I had to vow that we would never reveal the location to the outside world."

You cannot help but cheer aloud. You realize that you are about to see a village and a people that no one else in the world knows about!

Turn to page 108.

You open your eyes. You feel as if you're pulling yourself up from a deep cavern, climbing, climbing toward consciousness. Everything is a haze, a blur. The ground spins beneath you.

"Hey—he's coming to!" you hear a voice cry. It's Indy's voice.

Now Indy is standing over you. "You took a nasty hit on the head, kid," he says. "You've been out for hours. Can you see me?"

"Yes," you say. You have to struggle to speak. "I—can—see—you."

"Try to sit up," Indy says.

You pull yourself up. "I'm okay," you say, trying to ignore the throbbing in your head. "Wow, I had a fantastic dream!"

"Later, kid," Indy says. "Now that you're up, we've got to move away from here. There may be more rockslides. The Sherpas say we'll be a lot safer on higher ground. There are two paths from here. Either one of them will take us away."

You stand. You feel much better. Your eyes follow the two paths. One leads straight up the mountain; the other curves around it. Which will you choose?

....
The straight path? Turn to page 61.
The curved path? Turn to page 84.

One of the giants steps forward and calls out something in a strange language. Indy replies in the same language. They talk for several minutes, Indy still imprisoned in the furry arms of the yeti.

Finally Indy turns to you. "We've come too close to the Silver Tower and the giants' village," he says. "The yetis are the giants' guards. They'll crush us to death if we don't turn around and leave immediately."

The giants' leader calls out something else.

"We must also promise never to tell of what we have seen up here," Indy translates.

"No one would believe it anyway," George says, struggling to talk in the grasp of the yeti that holds him prisoner. "Promise them anything, Indy. Let's get away from here!"

Indy agrees. He speaks for a while to the leader of the giants. When the conversation is over, the giants turn and stride off across the snow. But the yetis continue to carry you. They carry you down the steep trail, several miles from where you met the giants. They finally set you down. Then they stand and watch as you continue down the trail toward Nepal.

"So close...yet so far," Indy mumbles sadly.

Indy is disappointed. But *you* have had the vacation of your life! Wait till the gang back home hears about all this! As you make your way home you are happy this adventure has come to

THE END!

31

"Wow! Look at the mountains down there!" you cry, staring out the tiny window.

"What did you say?" Indy asks.

The roar of the engine is so loud, he can't hear you across the tiny cabin.

"Storm coming up! Looks like a rough one!" the pilot calls back.

Everybody hears those words!

The plane lurches forward, then drops. A powerful wind batters it, turns it around, then pushes it upward again. The mountains seem to spin beneath you. The peaks grow larger as the plane loses altitude, drops, sputters, drops some more.

"I don't think we're gonna make it!" yells the pilot. "We've lost one engine!"

"Can you maintain any altitude?" Indy cries, ignoring the lurching of the plane and climbing up beside the pilot.

"I don't know. I just don't know!" the pilot shouts, panic in his voice.

Will you survive the storm?

Pick a number between one and ten.

....

If you picked an even number, turn to page 58.

If you picked an odd number, turn to page 66.

"Staying in this plane may be a good idea," Indy says, looking outside. "We seem to be in for a snowstorm."

You look out. The snow is falling so hard, it has already formed a light curtain over the plane windows. Soon sheets of snow are battering the small plane. This is not like the snowstorms back home!

"No one will be able to get through this snowstorm," says Lilah. "Let's face it, we're trapped here."

"I'm not so sure," Indy says, his face suddenly brightening. "I hear hoofbeats!"

You and Lilah run to the front of the plane to look out beside Indy. Through the falling snow you can just manage to see riders approaching. "I don't believe it!" Lilah cries happily. "We're saved! We're saved!"

Zzzzinnnnng!

A bullet flies over her head.

Zinnnnng. Zinnnnng.

"Duck back into the plane!" Indy cries. "They're shooting at us!"

Turn to page 47.

You run down the mountainside, practically flying over the snow. You fall, pull yourself up, and run again. Your companions are right behind you.

The roar of falling rocks and the rumble of the earth beneath you drown out the agonized screams of the giants, who are being crushed under tons of falling stone.

Moments later it is all over. The roar, the rumble, the cries—all silence now. The only sound you can hear is the crunch of your boots against the snow and the low whistle of the wind.

You return to the village. But there is no village to return to. The Silver Tower has fallen and crumbled. It is buried along with every trace of the giants and their homes.

"All gone," Indy says in a whisper. "All buried. These giants and their tower might never have existed. We certainly have no way to prove they did. They belong to legend now."

As you head slowly down the mountain Indy shakes his head and smiles. "You know what, kid?" he says. "No one would've believed us anyway!"

THE END

"I hope we get lucky," says Indy. "If they're bandits, we'll never be able to escape."

As the men come closer you see that they are wearing silver furs. They have olive skin and piercing black eyes. And they are at least eight feet tall!

"Giants!" Indy exclaims. "They really do exist!"

The leader steps forward and cries out angrily in a strange language, "Well this is lucky!" Indy mutters to you. "I know their language!" Indy steps forward to talk to the giant.

He returns a few moments later. "They're angry that we've intruded on them," Indy says. "But they are a kind people. They know we cannot survive here without their help. They have agreed to help us."

In the days to come the giants nurse George back to health. And they share with you the secrets of their people, the Silver Tower, and their lives in this isolated village. "Everyone seems so happy here," Indy tells you. "I don't know how to show these guys my gratitude."

Months later you arrive back in the United States and Indy takes you with him to the National Museum to see curator Marcus Brody. "Well?" Brody asks impatiently, ushering you into his office. "Well, Jones, what happened? Tell me everything."

Indy looks him in the eye. "We didn't find it, Marcus," he says. "There's no such thing as a Silver Tower. Just folklore. That's all it is."

THE END

"That snow will be down here in thirty seconds!" Indy cries.

"If we climb up on that rock ledge—" you start to say, watching the snow pick up speed above you.

"We can outrun it!" Lilah cries. "It will hit the ground in front of us—but it won't roll on this flat plateau! Run! Run back toward the plane!"

"There's no time to debate this!" Indy cries. And he's right.

You must make a fast decision—try to climb the rock ledge, or try to outrun the massive tons of falling snow?

If you choose the rock ledge, turn to page 52.

If you choose to run in the opposite direction turn to page 102.

"Good shooting, Lilah," Indy says, climbing slowly back up to his feet. Then another snake drops from a limb above him and falls to the ground near Indy's shoe. "Let's—uh—move away from these trees—FAST!" Indy cries.

The three of you begin to run.

You run over a carpet of reeds. The reeds give way beneath your feet. You begin to fall. Down, down into a pit—a hunter's animal trap!

You land with a *thud* fifteen feet below ground.

Indy groans and looks up at the darkening sky. "This just isn't our day," he mutters.

"Listen!" Lilah cries. "What's that sound?"

"Someone's coming!" you cry, hearing the crunch of footsteps on the jungle floor.

"We may be in very big trouble," Indy says, staring up at the top of the pit.

Turn to page 77.

"We thought we would freeze to death," Lilah continued. "We gave up hope. Then something amazing happened. We found ourselves standing in front of a gigantic tower, a tower made of silver, glowing against the mountains."

"Were you hallucinating?" Indy asked.

"That's what Dad and I thought," Lilah replied. "But the Silver Tower was real. It marked the entrance to a village. We were so weak and so frozen, we barely made it into the village. And Indy, it—it was a village—of GIANTS!

"The giants were at least eight feet tall. They were dressed for battle. They carried swords. At first they wanted to kill us. They didn't want any intruders. But then they saw what bad shape Dad and I were in. The fought over what to do with us. They were always fighting.

"Finally they decided to help us. They fed us and nursed us back to health. Then when we had recovered, they tied us up. They didn't want us to leave and tell others about their hidden village.

"But Dad worked out of his ropes. We escaped. We found a path down the mountainside. The next afternoon it started to snow. It was a real blizzard. Dad and I...we...we got separated. That was the last I saw of him. Somehow I...I made it back. But—" Lilah stopped and tried to fight back the tears.

"You've *got* to help me find him up there, Indy!" Lilah cried. "You're the only one I can turn to!"

Turn to page 40.

Indy removed his glasses and rubbed the bridge of his nose. "Lilah, that story about the Silver Tower and the giants—I've heard it many times before. It's just native folklore; you can't expect a scientist to believe it. There's no Silver Tower up there—it's probably a cliff that reflects the sunlight, a mirage caused by the reflection off the snow. And as for these giants—"

"I knew you might not believe me," Lilah said, her voice shaking. "But I've come prepared, Indy." She searched through her pocketbook and pulled out a silver coin. She held the coin up to Indy's surprised face. On one side of

40

it stood a tall, silver tower. "I took that from the giants' village," Lilah said.

Indy's face began to change. "Indy, you're the bravest man I know," Lilah said softly. "I know you can find Dad. I *know* it. And...if Dad could help us find the tower and the village again—think what it would mean to the museum!"

Indy knew she was right. To find a warlike tribe of giant humans, living untouched by the world in the shadow of a giant silver tower, would be an astounding discovery for the National Museum. A few minutes later Indy was on the phone to Marcus Brody, curator of the museum. A few minutes later Brody reluctantly agreed to pay for the trip. And a few minutes after that, you, Lilah, and Indy were on your way to Nepal—and the Himalaya Mountains!

To begin your journey into the mountains, turn to page 8.

Your arms hurt. You are gasping for breath.

"Keep digging," Indy cries, shoveling furiously. "I think we're making some progress."

But just as he says that, more snow falls from above. It fills the small tunnel you had managed to carve out.

"This is impossible," Lilah says, dropping the flat stone to the ground.

"Don't give up," George says. He picks up the stone and hands it back to her. "I didn't give up all the time I've been up in these mountains. You can't give up now!"

All four of you begin digging again with renewed energy. Soon you have carved out a small tunnel. "We're almost there," Indy says. "Almost there."

A few minutes later you break through.

"We're free!" you cry. "We did it! Now what?"

"Now we stay inside this cave!" Indy says.

Turn to page 55.

Earthquake Survival Tip #1: You can't hide from an earthquake.

And you can't hide from those massive rocks that are falling down onto the village from the cliffs above.

Quick—forget about finding cover.

Start running!

Turn back to page 35.

"They're riding too fast to be friendly," Indy
says. "Let's get moving!"

You run toward the river. "Look—a camp
down there!" you cry, pointing several hundred
yards downriver. "A camp—and a canoe!"

The three of you run across the hard snow,
slipping, falling, getting back up, running toward the canoe that is wedged into the snowy
riverbank. The camp is deserted. The boat is
yours!

Seconds later you are helping to push it
into the icy waters. You climb in. You bob up
and down, dodging chunks of ice as the small

canoe carries you downstream past scraggly trees and frozen terrain.

You see the horsemen behind you, at the riverbank. They are gesturing angrily. The river is carrying you away from them.

But wait. You seem to be slowing. The boat bumps into an ice block, seems to bounce backward, slows, bounces again.

The river is clogged with ice. You are trapped.

"Now what?" Lilah asks.

....

Turn to page 70.

"Indy, I really think we should see what it is," you insist.

The fire finally takes. Yellow and orange flames burst upward, filling the cave with warm light. "Okay, kid," Indy says. "Lilah, come with us. We'll see if we're sharing this cave with anybody. Then we'll come back and warm up."

The three of you climb up the gentle curve of the soft cave floor toward the entrance. Something darts quickly in front of you. It appears to run into another cave opening.

You follow it into the next cave. "Follow me!" you yell.

Indy and Lilah don't see anything.

Is it only a shadow?

Turn to page 60.

The horsemen gallop up to the plane. Their horses breathe thick white puffs of steam and snort noisily in the storm. The leader of the riders is wrapped in dark furs with a fur hood covering his face. All that you can see of his face is a bright red moustache. He starts to climb off his horse, a long rifle in his hand. He fires it into the air as his men dismount and begin to approach.

"Bandits!" Indy cries. "Let's get out of here!"

"Where can we run?" you cry, grabbing as many supplies as you can.

"I think there are trees over there," Indy says, pointing. "We can hide in the woods. Let's go!"

A few seconds later you are out of the plane and running as hard as you can. The bandits are after you, but their horses move slowly in the swirling snow.

"Keep running! We're almost there!" Indy cries.

But wait—where are the trees? Perhaps Indy just imagined them! The bandits are right behind you as the three of you realize that you have run right to the edge of a sheer drop-off!

Turn to page 67.

The snow comes down fast and wet. You slip and fall as you begin to make your way back down the narrow trail.

The wind blows the snow into your face. You pull yourself up, but trip and fall again.

Each time you fall, you pull Lilah down as well. She is tied by rope to you. Her father is behind her, secured by the same rope.

The drifts grow higher.

The trail is completely blocked.

"Someone is trying to tell us something, kid," Indy calls to you. "We have no choice but to climb higher and try to get out of this!"

Turn to page 89.

Indy rolls over on top of the tiger. It's taking all of his strength to keep the tiger pinned down.

The tiger roars in fury, its claws desperately scraping the air.

You spot Indy's pistol lying on the ground beside the tiger. Forgetting the danger, you lunge for it.

You grab the pistol and pick it up.

But you trip over a vine, and the gun flies out of your hands! It disappears behind a clump of bushes.

The tiger swipes a wide tear down the front of Indy's jacket with a quick motion of its forepaw. Then it lunges for Indy's shoulder, its sharp teeth gleaming—

Ka-zannnng.

A shot rings out.

Ka-zannnng.

Another.

Someone is shooting—at the tiger? Or at Indy?

Turn to page 54.

"I feel safer on foot," Indy says, motioning to the porters and Sherpas to get ready to move out. "If we can make it to the foothills by evening, we can set up camp there. Then, early in the morning, we can begin our climb into the mountains. Maybe the storms will hold off—"

Indy is interrupted by Mohaji. "May I have a word with you, sahib?" he asks.

"Yes. What's the matter?" Indy asks impatiently. He is eager to begin your long journey.

"There is trouble, sahib," Mohaji says, bowing his head. "I am most sorry to say that perhaps we will not be able to make this journey!"

What does Mohaji mean? Turn to page 14.

"There is only one way they will allow us to live," George continues. "If one of us can defeat their most powerful warrior, they will let us leave their village alive."

"I'm ready," Indy says, jumping to his feet. But then he sees the giants' most powerful warrior. "That guy is ten feet tall!" Indy cries.

Indy begins to follow the giant warrior toward the tower. "Indy—wait!" you call. You toss him his bullwhip.

"Thanks, kid," he calls as he follows the giant up the steps which lead to the top of the Silver Tower. "I'm going to need all the help I can get."

Indy and the giant disappear behind the tall, silvery tower. A few moments later they appear at the top, where the fight will take place. How can Indy ever defeat this powerful monster of a man? you wonder. You squint into the sun, watching every move at the top of the tower, knowing that your life depends on the outcome.

The giant lunges at Indy, trying to push him off the top of the tower. Indy dives under the giant's massive arm. All around you, the giants cheer for their warrior. Their shouting echoes off the mountains and becomes a deafening roar.

Then you watch in horror as the giant warrior lifts Indy high in the air. Will he toss Indy off the top of the tower?

Turn to page 13.

Indy is first to the ledge. He leaps up onto the jutting rock and raises his arms to pull himself higher. He finds a flat place, turns, and reaches down to help pull you up. Lilah pulls herself up beside you and Indy.

"Keep climbing," Indy says, pulling himself up higher. "We've got to go up a lot—"

But he is stopped in mid-sentence by the onrushing snow. The snow hits you with a *smack*. It pushes you off the rock ledge, pushes you away from your companions, pushes, pushes you faster and faster until you are drowning in a cold, wet wall of white.

. . . .
Turn to page 73.

"Do they look friendly to you, kid?" Indy asks. The four creatures are only a few yards away now.

"They're too tall to look friendly!" you cry.

Indy steps forward and holds up his right hand. "Hello!" he calls.

The yetis roar out a greeting. It is not friendly.

They do not stop to say hello. They run forward, roaring through huge teeth. They look half-human, half-ape, taller than both!

Indy reaches for his bullwhip, but a yeti knocks it down. Then the yetis pick the four of you up in their powerful arms and start running across the snow with you. Where are they taking you? And what will they do with you when you get there?

You cannot see—your head is covered by a furry arm.

Suddenly the yeti carrying you stops. You pull your head out from under his arm and see that you are surrounded—by men wrapped in fur jackets, wearing necklaces of animal teeth, and long braids. But the most striking thing about the men is their size. They're even taller than the yetis. They're giants!

"Help!" Indy calls out to them as the yetis growl in warning. "Can you help us?" he cries.

The giants stare at you in silence, their piercing black eyes expressionless. Can you stop the yetis? *Will* they?

Turn to page 31.

"Dad!" Lilah cries.

George Rogers steps out into the light and fires another shot at the tiger.

The tiger stops dead, then slumps to the ground. Indy rolls away from it and slowly climbs to his feet.

"Are you okay?" you cry, rushing over to him.

"A few scratches," he says. "Good shooting, George."

"I just happened to be in the neighborhood," Lilah's father says. "In fact, I've been wandering around this neighborhood for weeks!"

Lilah and her dad embrace. "I don't believe it. I just don't believe it!" she cries happily.

"I feel as if I've been living a dream all these weeks," George says. "I wandered down from the mountains and into the jungle. I really don't remember much about it. Then, a few days ago, I was in a village. The people were talking about a plane crash. I had to find out if you had come to rescue me and were in that plane. So I've been searching this accursed jungle since then. And now here you are! What a story I have to write when we get back!"

"I'm very interested in part of that story," Indy says. "George, can you lead us to the Silver Tower and the Village of the Giants?"

"The what???" asks George.

....
Turn to page 63.

54

Of course Indy is right. With night approaching, the cave is the warmest—and safest—place to be. You are so tired from your shoveling, you fall asleep in front of the fire before finishing your small dinner of dried beef.

The next morning you wake up, sore and aching from your night on the hard cave floor. Across from you, you hear Indy talking to George. "Can you lead us to the Silver Tower? Do you remember which direction it is from here?"

George is silent for a few moments. "Yes, I believe I can," he says.

That's all Indy has to hear. After a hurried breakfast, the four of you set off in the snow, George in the lead.

Two weeks later you are standing on a high cliff. The journey has been treacherous and exhausting. But it was worth all of the trouble. Just across a narrow valley, on a mountainside directly across from you, stands the Silver Tower! It glows so brightly that you are forced to shield your eyes.

"It's beautiful!" you cry.

"Let's go take a closer look," says Indy.

Turn to page 79.

You grab the sides of your seat so tightly that your hands turn white. Lilah's eyes are shut and her head is bowed.

The plane drops sharply. You both gasp. You watch Indy and the pilot shouting encouragement to each other in front of you. The pilot struggles desperately to control the throttle, which jerks and bounces in his hand as if it has a life of its own.

The other engine coughs once, twice, then resumes its roar. You look over at Lilah. You force yourself not to look out the window. Her eyes are still closed. A word forms on her lips: "Dad."

And then the plane crashes into a mountain peak, and everything goes black.

Turn to page 4.

Indy reluctantly agrees to change his plans and take the longer route through the mountains. Mohaji runs back to tell the Sherpas and porters.

As you begin your journey toward the foothills of the Himalayas, you pull your fur parka tighter around you and walk beside Indy.

"If your parents knew I'd dragged you here," Indy says, "they'd have my neck."

"I'll sure have some exciting stories to tell them when I get back," you say.

"I hope the stories aren't *too* exciting," Indy says.

You walk across the hard, rocky ground all afternoon. Finally, as the sun begins to lower itself behind the steep mountains, you reach the foothills.

You camp for the night. Sitting before the fire, you have your first taste of dried yak meat. It is a taste you will long remember.

The next morning you begin your climb up into the mountains. The going is slow, the mountain grows steep. You become surer of yourself as you continue to climb.

But then all of your confidence leaves you as you hear someone calling the dreaded word—"ROCKSLIDE!"

Turn to page 83.

"This way! I saw it again!" you say.

Indy and Lilah follow you. You leave one cave and find yourself in an even larger cave.

This cave leads to a smaller cave.

"I hope we can find our way back," Lilah says as you keep walking. "We could be wandering in these caves forever!"

Turn to page 90.

You begin to make your way up the straight path, walking ahead of the Sherpas and porters. As the path grows steeper you can hear the men muttering behind you.

"They're still talking about the rockslide," says Indy. "I hope nothing else goes wrong. These Sherpas have been known to desert a party if they feel bad luck is following them."

Just as Indy finishes these words you both look up at a small ledge a few yards above you—and see a large figure covered in fur!

Is it a yeti?

Indy draws his pistol. The large creature leaps off the ledge and stumbles toward you.

Turn to page 91.

61

"It's so beautiful up here," you say to Indy. "I've never seen browns and yellows like this!"

"Those browns and yellows will soon turn to white, kid," Indy says. "When we get up to the snow, you might not think it's so beautiful."

You travel smoothly and without stopping. You climb higher and higher. The trail grows steep and slippery.

By late afternoon the sun is a giant orange ball. You feel as if you are climbing right into it.

Suddenly a shadow crosses the sun. Then another.

What are these large creatures, black against the orange brightness, that are flying toward you?

"Hawks!" Indy yells. "Giant hawks! I think they're attacking!!"

Turn to page 74.

"Silver Tower? Giants? What are you talking about, Indy?" George asks, completely bewildered. You and Indy both turn to Lilah.

"I'm afraid I've got a confession to make," she says, hiding behind her father.

"Don't tell me," Indy says, closing his eyes tightly.

"Yes," Lilah says quietly. "We never found any giants or silver tower. I remembered the legend from a book. I—I lied to you, Indy. It was the only way I could get you to help me."

"Silver Tower?" George asks, still confused.

"Wait a minute—" you say. "What about the coin with the tower you showed Indy?"

"Remember? I didn't give you a good look at it. I never even let you hold it," Lilah says reluctantly. "But you were so excited by the whole idea, you hardly looked at the coin."

Lilah reaches into her coat pocket. She pulls out a silver coin and hands it to Indy. You walk over to take a close look at it.

The coin has a silver tower on one side. That's the side you saw. On the other side are the words "Souvenir of Silver Tower, Idaho, State Fair."

Lilah backs away warily, but Indy just grins.

"Lilah, you didn't fool me for a minute with that coin," he says. "I knew it was a fake all along. But I had to let you have your fun so that I could have mine!"

THE END

"I can't move! I'm sinking!" you cry out.

"Stop struggling!" Indy yells. "The more you struggle, the deeper you'll go."

"Thanks for the great advice. How about getting us out of here?" Lilah shouts.

Only your neck and head are above the surface. You watch Indy as he struggles to free his arm. With a final effort he pulls one arm free. The bullwhip slides off his shoulder.

"If I can loop it around one of those tall reeds, maybe I can pull myself out," Indy says. He swings the whip. It hits one of the dozens of tall, bent reeds that shoot out of the soft ground. But the reed cracks and falls.

"Try again," Lilah calls.

Indy takes aim and loops the whip out gently. This time it works. He wraps the whip around one of the reeds.

Indy pulls. Hard. Harder.

Slowly, he pulls himself out of the wet sand.

He quickly bends several reeds to the ground to make a rough platform. Then he pulls you and Lilah out. You are covered with thick, wet mud.

"We can go back to the plane and change our clothes," Lilah says. But then you see that the plane has nearly disappeared into the soft ground.

"There's a river," Indy says. "We could make a raft out of these reeds. It might be a faster way out of here."

What do *you* think?

....

Take the river? Turn to page 98.
Keep to the ground? Turn to page 115.

The second engine sputters. Then dies.

It's quiet now. Eerily quiet. Terrifyingly quiet.

The plane lurches forward.

Then it begins to drop.

You try to grab on to your seat. But there is nothing to hold on to.

Someone is screaming.

Is it you?

You feel as if you're floating now, floating up through the roof of the plane, up into the white, white mountains.

And then the white turns to black.

Turn to page 4.

Through the swirling snow, you see the bandits closing in, their rifles poised. The man with the red moustache is calling to you.

"We have no choice," Indy says. "We can't fight them."

"Do you mean we're going to jump off the cliff?" you ask.

"Ridiculous!" objects Lilah.

"Don't jump—try to slide," Indy says. "There's no way to tell how deep or steep it is in this snowstorm. Just try to slide on your back. Keep your legs and arms tucked in."

The bandits' rifle shots ring out. Bullets whiz above your heads.

"Happy landings!" Indy cries.

The three of you throw yourselves off the cliff and begin to slide—into the unknown!

Turn to page 87.

Indy finally gets the fire going. The flames leap up toward the cave ceiling, and the cave begins to glow with a warm, yellow light.

You decide Indy is probably right. You turn your eyes to the fire. You sit as close to it as you can. The warmth spreads slowly over your frozen skin. You close your eyes dreamily.

And when you open them, you see that the three of you are surrounded...

...by CAVEMEN! At least a dozen of them!

They have long, matted hair and wild, tangled beards that flow down to their waists. Dressed entirely in ragged animal furs, they begin to circle you, moving closer and closer!

Turn to page 104.

"We've gotta get back to shore," Indy says. "We'd better make a run for it. We're sitting ducks here in this boat!"

"How can we make a run for it across the water?" Lilah cries.

"Try to walk on the ice," Indy says, climbing out of the canoe and pulling her out after him. You climb out and try to get your balance on the big block of ice that has trapped the canoe.

"Just watch it," Indy says. He jumps onto the next chunk of ice, slips, then keeps going.

The three of you move as quickly as you can across the ice. River water splashes around you, covering your boots and churning around the deep ice blocks. You try to ignore it as you carefully make your way toward shore.

"Oops!" You fall. You are slipping, slipping into the cold water. A hand grabs your shoulder. Lilah pulls you back up onto the ice.

"Don't stop for a swim, kid," Indy calls. "We're almost there!"

One more block of ice. One more. You're on it now. You move one foot forward, then the other. You're there! You've all made it to shore.

"Hey—we're not alone!" Indy cries. A growling black bear, its teeth bared for attack, comes running toward you!

Turn to page 80.

"Ouch!"

"Ouch!"

"Ouch!"

Those scorpions can really sting, can't they?!

As you may have imagined from these cries of pain, Indy was not successful with his whip.

Fortunately, the Sherpas came running to your aid when they heard your desperate cries.

Unfortunately, you were in no shape to continue your journey.

Fortunately, they were able to carry you back to Nepal for medical treatment.

Unfortunately, that's the end of this adventure!

THE END

Snaaap!

Indy's whip cracks over the tiger's head.

The tiger stops short, looking confused.

Snaaap!

The whip cracks again over the giant animal's ear. Indy has his pistol in hand now.

Snaaap!

The tiger loses interest in you.

It turns toward Indy. It roars its anger.

It leaps onto Indy, throwing him down to the ground. The tiger opens its jaws, ready to taste victory.

Turn to page 49.

The three of you are sliding now, sliding on top of the rolling, falling snow as it begins to slow, then stop. You lie still, breathing so hard you feel you might burst. Your face is frozen. You cannot feel your hands.

"Hey—the ride's over!"

It's Indy calling to you. "We must've been on the tail end of it. That ride was smoother than a carnival merry-go-round!"

"Yeah, it must be our lucky day!" Lilah says less than enthusiastically.

"Look—a cave!" you cry.

They turn to where you're looking. "We seem to have fallen into a whole valley of caves," Indy says. "At least we know we'll have shelter for the night. Let's get a fire started. We'll have all the comforts of home."

"All the comforts of home," Lilah repeats, looking around this icy, dark valley of caves and shivering.

You walk behind Indy.

Was that someone—or something—moving around in the cave entrance? No. It must be your imagination...

Turn to page 86.

Indy raises his pistol and takes aim.

The giant beaks of these terrifying hawks are open. They squawk angrily as they fly right at you.

Indy is about to pull the trigger.

Suddenly Mohaji leaps onto Indy and pulls the pistol from his hand. "No, sahib!" he cries.

"Are you nuts?!" Indy yells. He dives to the ground for his pistol.

A hawk swoops down, lunges at Indy,

misses. The bird hits the rock behind Indy and, stunned, turns and flaps back up to the sky.

"I cannot allow you to shoot the sacred Giant Hawk!" Mohaji cries. He and Indy wrestle on the ground, each trying to get control of the pistol.

"This is ridiculous! Stop! Stop!" Lilah screams.

You reach down and grab the pistol off the ground. Indy and Mohaji continue to fight.

Ka-blaaaaam! Ka-blammmmmm!

Gunshots!

Is someone shooting at you??

Turn to page 118.

A man dressed in tattered furs steps out of the darkness. He is carrying a spear made from a cut-off tree limb.

"Dad!" Lilah cries.

George Rogers drops his handmade spear. His eyes open wide, first in disbelief, then in happiness.

"Dad! I don't believe it!" Lilah cries, rushing to him.

"We happened to be in the neighborhood, so we thought we'd drop by," Indy says, shaking George's hand.

"I've been searching these mountains for you," Lilah's father tells her. He cannot stop the tears that fill his eyes and run down his cheeks. "I had just about given up hope."

Lilah comforts her father. Indy turns to you and gives you the thumbs-up sign.

You are the first to hear the sound. It is a rumble. It grows louder, seems to shake the cave, then grows louder still. "Look!" you cry. "Snow! Snow has covered up the entrance to the cave! We're trapped!"

"The snow is still soft. We can dig our way out," George says.

"That could take days. Maybe we can find another opening to this cave," Indy suggests.

You must decide what to do.

. . . .

Try to dig your way out? Turn to page 85.
Look for another cave opening? Turn to page 93.

76

"Mohaji!" Indy cries.

The familiar face of the Sherpa leader peers down from the top of the animal pit.

"I think I can say without fear of contradiction that the three of us are very glad to see you," Indy says. "How did you ever find us?"

Mohaji and his men lower ropes and pull the three of you up to the ground. "We saw your plane go down, sahib. We followed your trail. We came as quickly as we could," the little man says with a wide grin. "It is only a few days' journey back to camp."

"Oh, Indy," Lilah says, "we'll go back to camp and be right back where we started."

"Not quite, missy," Mohaji says. "Just hours after your plane departed, a man wandered into camp. He is your father. He is not in very good shape, but he will soon be okay."

Lilah's grief turns to joy. "What are we waiting for?" she cries. "Let's head back to camp! And then it's back to the good old U.S.A.!"

"Uh—Lilah, aren't you forgetting about something? The Silver Tower?" Indy calls after her.

But she is so far ahead of him, she doesn't even hear him.

The Silver Tower, you realize, will remain just a legend—until you close the book and try a different path!

THE END

"Someone must've seen our plane crash," Lilah says. "They're coming to help us."

Indy watches them approach over the snow. "Hmmm...I'm not so sure they're friends," he says quietly. "These mountains are filled with tribes of bandits, bandits who would steal everything we have and leave us here with our throats cut."

"Look—on the other side of this rock ledge. There's a river," you tell Indy. "It isn't entirely frozen. Maybe we could use it to escape from them."

"But what if they're coming to help us?" Lilah asks. "Our chances of surviving out here on our own are pretty slim. They could be our only hope!"

You must quickly decide what to do.

Wait for the approaching riders and hope they're friendly? Turn to page 105.

Try to escape from them on the river? Turn to page 44.

78

You climb down the mountain and set up camp in the foothills overlooking the narrow valley. Every few minutes you look up and see the Silver Tower glowing above you, reaching into the clouds. It's beautiful—a seamless sheet of sparkling silver, smooth as glass, as wide and tall as a skyscraper.

"We're not dreaming it, kid," Indy says. "It's up there, all right."

The night passes peacefully. The next morning you begin to make your way across the narrow valley. It is warm in the valley, and the ground is soft, the first soft ground you have walked across since you began your trek through these mountains.

Soon you are climbing again, climbing the mountain that holds the amazing tower and the Village of Giants. "It's just a few hours' climb from here, I'd estimate," George says.

You climb for a few hours. "Say, the tower is...uh...a bit higher than I imagined," George says. You stop for a lunch of dried beef. You look up toward the cliff that holds the tower.

"Wait a minute! It looks just as far away as it did this morning!" you cry in surprise.

Can that be?

Turn to page 122.

The bear leaps onto Indy before Indy can get his pistol out. Indy falls over backward beneath the bear's massive weight.

Kaaa-channng. Kaaachannnnng!

Bullets ring out. The bear has been shot. It rears up on its hind legs, utters a painful cry of surprise, then keels over and hits the ground.

You turn around to see who fired the shots. It is one of the riders who were pursuing you. "They've caught up!" you cry to Indy, who is still dazed from the bear's attack.

"Lilah!" one of the riders cries.

"Dad! I don't believe it!"

"Lilah! I've been calling and calling to you! I guess you couldn't hear me over the horses' hooves! I've been searching these mountains for you with these men for weeks!" George Rogers cries. He jumps down from his horse and runs forward to hug his daughter.

The horsemen give a happy cheer as father and daughter are reunited. "I knew I'd find you. I *knew* it!" George cries happily. "Thank you, Indy, for your help!"

"It was nothing," Indy says quietly, still examining the damage the bear did to his fur parka. "Maybe you can return the favor now. Can you lead us to the Village of Giants?"

"I can," says George. "But I won't."

Turn to page 106.

Closer and closer come the yaks. The ground shakes so hard, you find it difficult to stand.

In the corner of your eye you see a tall rock ledge to your right. "The rocks!" you scream over the thundering hooves of the approaching beasts. "Maybe we can climb them!"

But Indy already has his pistol in his hand. "These shots will scare them and make them turn away!" he cries.

Which is a better way to survive this stampede—try to climb the rock ledge? Or fire shots to make them change their direction?

You decide.

If you choose the rock ledge, turn to page 97.

If you choose the pistol shots, turn to page 16.

The rocks bounce and crack as they roll down the mountainside above you. "Quick!" Indy cries. "Duck under that rock ledge over there! We'll be safe—"

But it is too late. You cannot run for cover fast enough. The rocks are falling all around you.

"AAAIIIII!"

Who is that crying out in pain?

It is *you*.

You've been hit by a rock!

Turn to page 95.

"This mountain trail seems to lead away from the rockslide area," Indy says as you take to the curved path, walking ahead of the Sherpas and porters. Indy keeps his eyes on the cliffs above. "How are you feeling, kid?" he asks.

"I feel as if I have a rock for a head," you tell him, still a bit dizzy as you make your way up the snowy mountain.

"You must have a head as hard as a rock to survive that direct hit!" Indy says.

You hear a noise from a ledge above, and the three of you look up to see if you can determine what caused it. For a split second you take your eyes off the pathway in front of you.

And in that split second you fall into a pit that lies in the center of the path.

You land at the bottom of the pit, about ten feet below the ground.

"I think we've got trouble here," Indy says, his face frozen in fear. "This pit is filled with SCORPIONS!"

Turn to page 92.

"Let's try to dig before the snow gets packed hard," George insists.

"We can't dig without shovels," says Lilah.

"I saw some flat stones on the cave floor," you say. "We can dig with them."

"Good idea, kid," Indy says. "Go get 'em."

A few moments later the four of you are digging out the snow that holds you prisoner. The snow is packed harder than you imagined. And as soon as you make a little progress, as soon as you get a few feet of tunnel dug out, more snow falls in its place and you have to start again.

"Let's rest for a bit. I'm exhausted," George says.

"We can't stop," Indy says. "If the snow freezes, we'll be trapped forever."

Will you be able to dig your way out of this frozen prison? There is only a fifty-fifty chance that you can.

Pick a number between one and 10.

....

If you picked 3, 5, 6, 8, or 10, turn to page 117.

If you picked 1, 2, 4, 7, or 9, turn to page 12.

85

You run out of the cold and into the shelter of the cave. Indy struggles to make a fire. It is windy even in the depths of this cave, and the tiny flame keeps blowing out.

You look into the darkness. Again, you see someone—or something—dart into the shadows.

"Indy, I don't think we're alone," you say quietly. Your voice echoes off the cave walls. Even a whisper is carried and repeated through the cave. "I saw something move."

Indy and Lilah both look up. There is nothing to be seen now.

"Just shadows," Indy says.

You hear a crunching sound, the sound of a foot on packed snow.

"Shadows don't make noise, do they?" you ask.

"No, but the wind does," Indy replies. "Calm down, kid. There are probably some animals in this cave. But they have a right to be here too."

Should you ignore what you saw—or go investigate? You must decide.

If you choose to ignore it, turn to page 68.
If you choose to investigate, turn to page 46

Down, down you tumble, picking up speed as you fall. You lose control and begin to roll over and over, but the deep snow acts as a cushion, and its softness keeps you from serious injury.

You land sooner than you think. The cliff was not a tall one.

"That was a good ride. And we didn't even have to buy a ticket," Indy says, standing up and brushing snow from his parka.

"Are we dead or alive?" Lilah asks.

"We're alive," Indy says. He pulls her up out of the deep drift she's landed in. "And we've given the slip to those bandits."

"Look!" you cry, pointing. Your fall has landed you right at the entrance to a large cave. "Maybe we can spend the night inside."

"Maybe..." Indy says, staring through the snow into the dark cave opening. "Or maybe not. I just saw something move in there. Someone—or something—is already living inside that cave!"

Turn to page 109.

"We've come this far. We'll find that tower," Indy cries as you climb up, up, up against the snow. Suddenly Indy shouts, "Look out!"

But his warning is too late.

You slip in the snow and slide down several hundred yards. The rope around your waist snaps tight and you stop falling. You are suspended in air, dangling from the rope. Slowly, slowly, Indy pulls you back up.

"Are you sure we made the right choice?" you ask, gasping for breath. "Maybe we should turn back now!"

"We're almost above the storm," Indy says. "We'll climb a little higher and we should be okay."

"Okay?" Lilah cries. "Okay?!? Stranded out here without Sherpas? Wandering in the snow?!"

"We're due for some good luck," Indy says without cheer.

"Hey—who's *that*?!" you cry, pointing to a tall figure running toward you through the snow. "It looks like—like—"

Like a yeti!

At least it looks like the yetis in the picture books you've seen!

Is it possible? Were the Sherpas right after all?

....
Turn to page 103.

"Well, kid, are you satisfied?" Indy asks as the three of you stare at the dark walls of an empty cave.

"I *know* I saw something?" you insist. "Maybe if we go a little farther—"

"We've already gone too far," Indy says. "I just hope Lilah isn't right. I just hope we don't spend the rest of our days wandering through these miserable caves!"

Are you trapped in the caves *forever*?

Turn to page 60.

"Don't shoot!" the approaching creature yells.

Indy keeps his pistol pointed but doesn't fire.

"Lilah—is that you?" the creature yells.

As Lilah rushes forward to hug the approaching figure, it becomes clear that this is no yeti. It is George Rogers, wrapped in furs for protection against the frozen winds of the mountains.

"I don't believe it! I've found you!" Rogers cries happily. "Indiana Jones," he says, throwing out his hand to grasp Indy's. "Is it really you, or is it a mirage?"

"I *feel* like a mirage after this trip," Indy says. "You have a brave daughter, Rogers. She—"

Indy doesn't continue. You all see riders approaching, bringing their horses up the steep path at breakneck speed. "There seem to be hundreds of them!" you cry, looking at Indy to see what to do next.

The Sherpas and porters flee, running from the path in several directions. You hear rifle fire, and bullets whiz over your head.

"The riders are bandits!" Rogers cries.

Turn to page 101.

"Help!" Lilah screams. "Where are the Sherpas? Where's Mohaji?"

Indy clamps a hand over her mouth. "Don't scream," he whispers. "Don't move. It'll excite the scorpions!"

"Excite *them*?" Lilah cries, pushing away his hand. "What about *us*?!"

Scorpions crawl over your boots. One starts to crawl up your leg.

"Do they bite?" you ask, nervously.

"They don't bite," Indy says, brushing two of them off his sleeve. "They sting. And believe me, kid, if you get stung by one of these beauties, you'll wish they *did* bite!"

"I think I have to scream," Lilah says.

Can you get out of this scorpion pit?

Turn to page 99.

You search and search, until your body aches and your head throbs. Finally Indy turns to you in the darkness. "Well, that settles that," he says, unable to hide the disappointment in his normally steady voice. "There's no other opening to this cave. We've searched every inch!"

Looks like you made a bad choice. But don't give up hope. You still may be able to dig yourself out of this mess.

Turn to page 85.

"No! It can't be!" you shout.

Indy steps forward on top of the tower, raising his arms in triumph. He has defeated the giant warrior!

"How did he do it? How?!?" George asks happily.

"If the giants keep their promise, we'll soon be free!" you cry.

A few minutes later you are free. The four of you are walking as quickly as you can down the mountain trail away from the Village of Giants.

"Indy, this is impossible!" you say. "There was no way you could defeat that giant. He picked you up like you were a stuffed toy!"

"I know," Indy says mysteriously. "There was no way I could win."

You walk on a little farther. "Come on, tell us how you did it!" you plead.

"It was quite simple, really," Indy says, pleased with himself. "The giant had one little weakness."

"What? What was it?" you ask.

"He was ticklish," says Indy, grinning.

You all begin to laugh at this impossible victory. It could only happen to Indiana Jones!

THE END

"Are you okay, kid?" Indy asks, leaning over you. He's dabbing your forehead with a wet cloth.

You look up to see if the rocks are still falling. They've stopped. "I'm fine—I guess," you say groggily.

"Yeah, you look okay to me," Indy says. He motions to the Sherpas. "Let's get moving again!"

He pulls you to your feet. "Pull your hood up over your head, kid," he tells you. "You'll be fine."

A few moments later you are climbing again, pulling yourself up to a ledge, and then looking down at the foothills far beneath you.

You find yourself on a windswept plateau. It begins to snow, and the wind lashes the wet snow against your frozen face. Then, through a cold white blur, you see large creatures running toward you.

They are taller than humans—as tall as giraffes. They are bright green. They lift their heads to the gray sky and roar—and fire flames from their throats.

DRAGONS???

....
Go on to page 96.

"Stand back!" you cry to Indy and Lilah. "I'll take care of these dragons!"

You grab Indy's bullwhip from his shoulder and run toward the charging dragons. They shoot hot walls of fire out in front of them. The Sherpas and porters flee in terror.

You stand and face them. They are only a few yards away from you now. You raise the bullwhip.

"Stop, kid!" Indy cries.

But he is too late. You crack the whip in the air. Once. Twice.

The dragons stop in their tracks.

"Get back!! Back!" you scream. You crack the bullwhip again.

The dragons turn and flee.

"Hey, kid, that was tremendous!" Indy says with admiration.

"Look over there!" you cry, pointing to a tall cliff just ahead of you. "We've found it already!"

Sure enough, shining against the afternoon sky stands the Silver Tower!

Turn to page 5.

The three of you scramble up the rocks as fast as you can. The stampeding yaks are only a few yards away now. They kick up the snow beneath their hooves until the air is filled with fine white powder.

Lilah is the first to get to the top of the ledge. "Hurry!" she cries. "Hurry!"

It isn't really necessary for her to yell that.

You get to the top of the rocks just in time. Their eyes red and frightened, the yaks go running past. Then, gradually, the roar of their hoofbeats fades away, the snow they kicked up into the air settles slowly to the ground, and all is peaceful again. You, Indy, and Lilah are alone.

Or are you?

"Men are approaching on horseback!" Indy cries. "And they're riding fast!"

Turn to page 78.

The three of you work for several hours to build a raft from the jungle reeds. You are exhausted by the time it's finished.

You wash yourselves off in the cold water and then climb on to the raft. It glides easily and rapidly downriver.

Staring up at the long, curved branches of the jungle trees as you float beneath them, you feel strangely calm and satisfied. And you feel hopeful.

These feelings, unfortunately, are not destined to last.

If you knew the name of this river, you would not be so calm.

The river, you see, is known to everyone but you as "The River of the Hidden Waterfall."

In a few moments the Hidden Waterfall will no longer be hidden from you. And your river ride will become a lot more exciting—so exciting, in fact, that it will bring this brief adventure to

THE END!

"Lilah's right. Where are the Sherpas?" you ask.

"I can't call to them without getting these scorpions worked up," Indy whispers, gently kicking a scorpion off his ankle and onto the pile of scorpions beneath his boots. A scorpion raises its tail as if to sting, but then settles back.

"I know why the Sherpas won't come near us," Lilah says. "If this is our fate, they don't want to disturb us. My father warned me about mountain people and their superstitions."

"Let's change our fate," Indy says, pulling the bullwhip off his shoulder. "Maybe there's something at the top of the pit that I can hook this whip on. Then we can pull ourselves out of this hole!"

Softly, softly, he arches the whip and tosses it up toward the top of the pit. Will you be able to pull yourself away from a stinging death?

There's only a small chance—but it's your only chance.

If you're reading this book on a Saturday, Sunday, Monday, or Friday, turn to page 112.

If you're reading this on any other day, turn to page 71.

"We seem to be trapped here," Indy says, looking around for an escape route.

"Is that a cliff over there?" you ask, pointing a few yards to the right of the mountain path.

The four of you run toward it, keeping low to dodge the bullets. The bandits are right behind you now.

"It's some sort of crevasse," Indy yells. "Quick—slide down!"

You throw yourselves down the steep incline. You slide down into a narrow opening in the ground. The bottom leads out to a valley filled with snow and white rocks. "Stay against the side! " Indy cries.

Above you the bandits look down into the crevasse. You wait in silence. Will they pursue you—or will they go on?

You can hear the snorting of impatient horses above you. You try to press yourself into the cliff wall.

After what seems like hours, you hear the horses turn and gallop away in the snow. The bandits have decided it isn't worth following you down the crevasse.

Still pressed against the cliff wall, you look across the narrow valley. The valley ends at another steep cliff wall. And standing high above, you see the Silver Tower!

Turn to page 6.

Mountain Climbing Lesson #1: You can't outrun an avalanche.

THE END

The four of you stand frozen on the trail, watching the large, fur-covered creature approach.

"No!" Indy yells over the howling wind. "It's not a yeti!"

You breathe a sigh of relief.

"It's *four* yetis!" Indy cries.

The creatures are running single file across the snow-covered trail.

"How interesting!" George cries. "We must go up and try to greet them. This is an incredible opportunity!"

"I'd rather see them in the movies!" Lilah shouts. "Let's run!"

What do *you* choose to do—stay and try to greet them? Or run for your life?

....
If you choose to greet them, turn to page 53.
If you choose to try to escape from them, turn o page 119.

As always, Indy has his bullwhip right beside him. He raises it high over his head. But before he can bring it down, one of the primitive-looking men leaps at him.

Indy falls backward onto the cave floor. He and the large, snarling caveman wrestle as the other cavemen look on, jumping up and down and screaming in excitement.

Indy's whip lies a few yards away from him on the cave floor. You dive for it and pick it up. You raise it high. Maybe you can crack it in the air and frighten these strange-looking men into retreating.

But before you can do anything with the whip, a caveman leaps down from his perch above you and grabs the whip out of your hand. The caveman tosses the whip away and turns to fight *you*!

Lilah screams.

Turn to page 111.

"Let's hope these riders are friendly," Indy says, raising his arms in greeting to them. "Otherwise, I'm going to feel like a real fool!"

The riders wave back. They ride up to the rock ledge you are standing on and stop.

"They're friendly," you say. "Look—they're offering us food." From bags on their saddles, they bring out sticks of dried mutton.

Indy tries to talk to them, but he doesn't know their language. He gestures and makes hand signs. After a while they grin and seem to understand.

"I think I've gotten through to them," Indy says. "They're going to lead us through these mountains to the Tibetan side."

You begin the journey immediately, sharing the saddles with your rescuers. Sometimes the trail becomes too steep or too narrow to ride, and you help to lead the horses down the treacherous mountains, down, down, through the deep, blowing snows.

The journey takes several days. It isn't until you reach a small town and are greeted by the people there that you realize these horsemen have led you in the wrong direction.

They did not understand Indy after all. They have led you back to Nepal!

How will you ever get to the other side of the mountains? Close the book and try again!

THE END

"George, I'm not sure I heard you correctly," Indy says. "This village may be the greatest find of the century."

"It is the greatest find of the past four centuries," George says. "But I will not help you find it. The village and the Silver Tower must remain only a legend. There have been no intruders there for four thousand years. I will not be responsible for destroying the villagers' way of life."

Indy is silent for a long while. "Let's start back to Nepal," he says finally.

"You won't go back empty-handed," George says. "Cheer up, Indy. Here's a present for you, something I took from the giants' village. I think you'll find it of great interest."

He hands Indy an ancient silver knife. "The giants are great warriors and great silver-smiths," George says. "Look at the intricate carving on the handle. Look at how the silver glows, almost as if it is alive! You'd never guess this knife was four thousand years old!"

"It must be worth millions!" Indy cries, gently taking the knife, turning it over and over in his trembling hands.

"It is yours for reuniting me with my daughter," George says. "Now, let's begin our journey home."

THE END

The next few days are a time of exciting exploration and discovery. "Look how they've provided for all their needs on this mountain plateau!" Indy exclaims in admiration. "That irrigation system is as advanced as any I've seen. And it allows them to grow all the food they need even at this high altitude."

The four of you are amazed by the artwork of these giant people—silver carvings, ornate woven tapestries. And you cannot help but see how they live so well together in peace and harmony. "This is amazing! Just amazing!" Indy keeps crying happily, his enthusiasm as strong as his scientific curiosity.

Then, on the third day of your visit in the Village of Giants, your explorations are interrupted.

The ground begins to shake. Rocks begin to fall from the cliffs above the village. The giants' houses begin to crack apart and fall.

"EARTHQUAKE!" you shout. You begin to run down the trail that leads away from the village. Indy, Lilah, and her father are somewhere behind you.

"No—don't run! Take cover!" you hear someone call.

You must decide what to do.

....

Run from the village? Turn to page 35.
Take cover inside the village? Turn to page 43.

"Well, we can't stand out here and freeze," Indy says. "We have no choice but to go into that cave and see if whatever or whoever's in there is friend or foe!"

Indy draws his pistol, and the three of you make your way across the deep snow to the entrance of the cave. "I don't see a doorbell," Indy says, peering into the darkness. "So I guess we'll just invite ourselves in." You take several reluctant steps into the dark cave.

"Stop right there!" cries a husky voice. "Don't come any closer!"

Turn to page 76.

The vultures fly in a low circle above your heads.

"They must wait around here for the scorpions to do their job," Indy says, watching the large birds dart and swoop. "Don't worry about them. They won't attack anything that's still alive. We've cheated them out of dinner—this time!"

Suddenly Mohaji, leader of the Sherpas, stands before you.

"Where the heck have you been?!" Indy asks angrily.

"Bad omens follow this expedition, sahib," Mohaji says, ignoring Indy's question. "We must go back to our village now. The fates do not wish us to continue." Before Indy can reply, Mohaji has turned and gone back to the other Sherpas.

You watch as they quickly make their way back in the direction from which you've come. "This is horrible!" Lilah cries. "We can't get through these mountains without them!"

You have no time to think about your predicament. Running toward you across the snow is a man, waving his arms and screaming against the wind!

Turn to page 7.

The primitive man stops. He stands staring, frozen in front of you.

Lilah screams again.

Indy's attacker also freezes. The caveman leaps away from Indy.

"Lilah, you may have to keep screaming for a while," Indy says, slowly picking himself up off the ground. "It seems to have a good effect on these Neanderthal types!"

Lilah screams again, enjoying it this time.

The cavemen back up against the wall.

"One more time," Indy calls to her.

But Lilah doesn't scream again. She is staring at the far end of the cave. A figure emerges from the darkness.

"I don't believe it!" Lilah cries. "Dad!"

Go on to page 114.

You watch the whip sail up to the top of the pit. You concentrate all your energies on it and away from the crawling creatures at your feet. Will it catch on something up there?

No.

It falls back to the floor of the pit.

Indy pulls it up again, tries once more. Will it catch?

Yes.

He tugs at it.

Yes.

"Up you go," he says, lifting Lilah out of

the tangle of scorpions that cover her boots.
"Climb. Climb as fast as you can."

Lilah scampers up the rope.

You are next. You try to pull yourself up.
"This isn't as easy as it looks," you say.

"Hurry up, kid," Indy says. "I want to get
outta here, too, ya know?"

A few seconds later all three of you are up
at the top, looking down into the scorpion pit.
Suddenly the sky darkens. A flock of huge black
birds swoops down toward you.

"VULTURES!" Lilah cries.

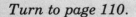

Turn to page 110.

113

The cavemen stand and watch in silence as Lilah and her father are reunited. "Don't hurt these good fellows," George Rogers tells Indy. "They took care of me all of the weeks I've been stranded up here. They aren't vicious. They were just trying to protect me from you."

"It's good that you make friends so easily, George," Indy says. "Otherwise you would've been a dead duck up here."

"It was rather a close call," Lilah's father says, his arm around Lilah's shoulder. "But I knew that Lilah would find a way to rescue me."

After a warm dinner by the fire, Indy brings up the second part of your mission in the Himalayas. "Can you lead us to the Silver Tower?" he asks George.

"When do you want to leave?" George asks. "Right now—or in the morning?"

You decide.

....

If you choose to leave right now, turn to page 3.

If you choose to wait till morning, turn to page 11.

"On second thought, there's no telling where that river leads," Indy says. "Let's stay on the bank and follow it upstream as far as we can. The higher we get, the better our chances of leaving this jungle behind."

The three of you wash yourselves off in the cold water of the jungle river. Then you walk along the bank, pulling yourself over the wet, muddy ground by holding on to the reeds and tree roots that cover the ground.

Walking on such uncertain terrain is frightening—and exhausting. As the late afternoon sun begins to lower behind the trees, your pace slows, your legs ache, your chest heaves. "Keep moving, keep moving," Indy commands. "There's no place here to stop and—"

All three of you look up at the same time.

What are those things dangling from the low tree branches above your heads? Has someone tied ribbons around the branches?

Suddenly one of the ribbons drops onto Indy's shoulder.

You all see immediately that it is not a ribbon.

It is a snake!

Another one drops from its high perch. Then another!

"Oh, no! Not snakes!" Indy cries, his eyes wide with terror. "I can take *anything* but snakes!"

. . . .

Turn to page 116.

You didn't think it possible. But Indy is actually paralyzed with fear!

A snake is perched on his shoulder. It rears back its narrow head, its black eyes glowing in the dying afternoon sunlight, and opens its mouth wide to reveal its glinting fangs.

Indy doesn't move.

He doesn't seem able to move.

Another snake drops off a low tree limb, just missing your shoulder. A snake lands on Lilah's head. She slaps it away.

Quickly, Lilah moves forward, grabs Indy's pistol from its holster at Indy's waist, and fires pointblank at the snake on Indy's shoulder.

Indy falls to the ground.

Has Lilah shot him?

Turn to page 38.

You dig with the flat stones till you can barely raise your arms.

"The snow is getting harder!" Lilah cries.

"Keep scraping away at it," Indy commands. He digs at the snow ferociously. You try to dig as fast as he does, but your arms are tired and your heart is pounding.

Snow falls into the small tunnel you've managed to dig. "Keep trying, keep trying!" Indy cries. But he is the only one who can continue. The rest of you are too exhausted to go on.

Indy digs for another twenty minutes. Then he too gives up. He tosses the flat stone angrily at the cave wall.

"Do you believe in miracles?" Indy asks you. "I hope so, kid. Because that's what it's going to take to free us from this miserable cave!"

Just then, you hear voices from outside. And you hear the sound of shovels digging away at the snow that blocks the cave entrance.

"Someone has found us!" you cry. "We're saved! It *is* a miracle!"

Is it? Turn to page 24.

"Dad!" Lilah cries.

George Rogers stands on the ledge above you. "I've found you!" he cries happily.

"No! We've found *you*!" Lilah cries, running to him.

Indy and Mohaji stop their fight. The hawks circle. The gunshots have scared them off.

Mohaji gets up and walks directly to his men. A few seconds later the Sherpas are making their way down the trail, back to Nepal. They have deserted.

"Finding you is a stroke of luck," George says, greeting Indy warmly.

"But now we may be together up here for a very long time," Indy says grimly, watching the Sherpas head down the mountain. "Can you lead us to the Silver Tower and the village of giants?"

"I'm not sure," Lilah's father says. "I've been wandering up here for so long..."

A heavy snow starts to fall. The air grows colder. You pull your fur parka around you more tightly. Indy secures all four of you together by tying ropes around your waists.

"Well, we've found you," Lilah says. "Maybe we should just head back. Look how fast this snow is piling up!"

You decide. Head back—or risk the snow and search for the tower?

....

If you choose to head back, turn to page 4.

If you choose to challenge the snowstorm and keep going, turn to page 89.

118

"Run!" Indy cries.

But he doesn't need to tell you that.

The four of you are running across the snow.

You slip and fall. You pull yourself back up.

You look back. The yetis are gaining on you.

"They're too fast!" you cry. "We can't outrun them!"

"Stop! This is ridiculous! He's right!" Lilah cries.

The four of you stop running.

You turn to face the four giant, fur-covered creatures.

"We have no choice," Indy says, his hand on his pistol. "Let's try to make nice, gang." He forces a smile to his lips. "And if that doesn't work..." He doesn't finish his sentence.

Will they be friendly? Turn to page 53.

119

"We'll be there by nightfall," Indy says quietly. But there is doubt in his voice.

You begin to climb again. The mountain grows steep. You move much more slowly, pulling each other up by rope.

As evening approaches you look up toward the Silver Tower. "We're not any closer!" you cry weakly.

"Impossible," George says.

"Ridiculous," mutters Lilah.

"The kid's right," Indy says. "Something funny is going on here."

You stop and make camp. The next day you begin your climb again. You climb all day, and still you come no closer to the magical tower above.

You climb for a third day. As evening approaches you realize that the tower is just as far from you as when you began your climb.

Is the tower real? Is it an illusion? Is it magic?

You realize that you will never get close enough to find out.

You head down to the narrow valley. You're on your way home. You don't look back. You journey has come to

THE END.